Rory Learns a Lesson

A Story of Family

Published in 2010 by Windmill Books, LLC
303 Park Avenue South Suite # 1280, New York, NY 10010-3657

Adaptations to North American Edition © 2010 Windmill Books

First published in Great Britain in hardback in 2001 by Brimax Publishing Ltd
First paperback edition published in Great Britain in 2002 by Brimax Publishing Ltd
Appledram Barns, Birdham Road, Chichester, PO20 7EQ, UK
© Brimax Publishing Ltd

CREDITS:
Author: Gill Davies, Illustrator: Rachael O'Neill

Library of Congress Cataloging-in-Publication Data

Davies, Gill, 1946-
 [Rory's story]
 Rory learns a lesson : a story of family / text by Gill Davies ; illustrations by Rachael O'Neill. -- North American ed.
      p. cm. -- (Let's grow together)
 "Alphabet Soup."
 Summary: Although Rory the tiger is not very happy to have a new baby sister, he finds that she is nicer than he thought.
 ISBN 978-1-60754-759-4 (library binding) -- ISBN 978-1-60754-767-9 (pbk.) -- ISBN 978-1-60754-768-6 (6-pack)
 [1. Sibling rivalry--Fiction. 2. Babies--Fiction. 3. Brothers and sisters--Fiction. 4. Tigers--Fiction.] I. O'Neill, Rachael, ill.
 II. Title.
 PZ7.D28387Ror 2010
 [E]--dc22
              2009035884

Manufactured in China

CPSIA Compliance Information: Batch #PW01W: For further information contact Windmill Books, New York, New York at 1-866-478-0556.

Let's Grow Together

Rory Learns a Lesson

A Story of Family

Text by Gill Davies
Illustrations by Rachael O'Neill

alphabet
soup ™

an imprint of
WINDMILL BOOKS™
New York

Rory the tiger is having a terrible time!
He has a new *baby sister*.
She is very small and cries a lot, and
she waves little, clenched paws in the air.
Rory does not know what to think of her.
She is too small to play with him.
He is afraid to hold her in case she slips.
Now his mother and father are always busy.

"Will you cuddle me?" asks Rory.

"In a minute," says Mother Tiger.

"First I have to feed the baby."

Rory waits...

"Will you cuddle me now?" asks Rory.

"Soon," says Mother Tiger.

"First I have to wash the baby's ears."

Rory waits...

"Will you give me a ride on your back?"
asks Rory.
"Soon," says Mother Tiger.
"First I have to wash the baby's face."
Rory waits...
"Will you give me a ride on your
back now?" asks Rory.
"Soon," says Mother Tiger.
"First I have to wash the baby's tail."
Rory sighs and goes to see if his father
will play with him.

"Will you climb a tree with me?"
Rory asks Father Tiger.
"Soon," says Father Tiger,
"but first I have to finish cleaning the den."
Rory waits...

"Will you climb a tree now?"
asks Rory.
"Soon," says Father Tiger. "First I have
to teach the baby how to growl.
Do you want to help?"
"No," says Rory, feeling a little bit
left out, and sad, and bored.
Everyone is so busy.

Rory goes outside. Hippo comes
bouncing along the path.
"Hi!" says Hippo.
"Want to play a game?"
"Okay," says Rory, grinning,
"what do you want to play?"

Crocodiles!

They have a fun game!

First Hippo pretends to be a crocodile chasing Rory.

Then Rory pretends to be a crocodile chasing Hippo.

The two friends run in circles until they fall over, laughing and kicking their legs in the air. They pretend to SNAP! big crocodile teeth. SNIP SNAP! Growwwl!

Mother Tiger opens the door,
looking angry.
"Ssshh, you two!" she says.
"You are making too much noise.
You will wake the baby...
listen, she is crying already."

Mother Tiger goes back indoors.
Rory and Hippo can hear
the little cub crying, but after
a while the sound stops.

"Let's take a look," says Hippo,
"I haven't seen your new baby sister yet."
So they tiptoe inside.
Mother Tiger is holding the baby
and singing softly to her.

"Hush little tiger, don't growl and cry,
Mama's going to sing you a lullaby.
The jungle is green, the sky is blue,
Your brother Rory wants to cuddle you."

"No I don't!" says Rory.

"I don't know how."

"It's easy," says Mother Tiger.

"Sit down and I'll show you."

Mother Tiger brings the baby over to Rory.

Suddenly, there is Rory's new baby sister,

all cuddled up on his lap.

She feels warm and soft. She smiles.

Rory smiles back.

"You're nice," says Rory.
His baby sister makes a gurgly growl back.
She clasps his paw tight. Then she closes her
eyes and falls asleep. Mother Tiger puts the
baby back into her snug corner of the den.

Rory and Hippo creep back outside
to play a quiet game.
"My baby sister's not so bad,"
says Rory to Hippo.
"She's cute," says Hippo.
"You're lucky, Rory."

Now Rory tells everyone in the jungle
about his new baby sister.
"She's soft and warm!" he says.
"She can clench her fists!" he smiles.
"And she's got a gurgly growl," he grins.
Then he practices his own lullaby
to sing to his little sister.

"Hush little sister, don't cry at all,
Rory will hold you so you won't fall.
The jungle is green, the sky is blue,
Your brother Rory is proud of you."

LEARN MORE!

Rory is a pretend tiger. Here are some fun facts so you can learn more about real tigers.

- Did you know that a group of tigers is called a streak?
- A tiger may take several days to finish eating an animal it has killed. The tiger will eat its fill, then cover the dead animal with leaves and dirt to hide it from other predators. When the tiger is hungry, he will come back for more.
- Tigers like the water, and will often soak in streams to cool off.
- No two tigers have the same pattern of stripes.
- Would you believe that a tiger's roar can be heard from almost two miles (3.2 km) away?

For More Information

This story is about tigers and welcoming a new family member. Check out the books and Web sites below to learn more about tigers, or what you can do if you are feeling like Rory!

Books

Edom, Helen and Robert Morton. Why do tigers have stripes? Eveleth, MN: Usborne Books, 2006.

Harvey, Tom and Allie Harvey. Tiger pups. New York: Collins, 2009.

Kuklin, Susan. Families. New York: Hyperion, 2006.

Skutch, Robert. Who's who in a family. Berkeley, CA: Tricycle Press, 2004.

Web Sites

To ensure the currency and safety of recommended Internet links, Windmill maintains and updates an online list of sites related to the subject of this book. To access this list of Web sites, please go to www.windmillbooks.com/weblinks and select this book's title.

For more great fiction and nonfiction, go to
www.windmillbooks.com.